# PIXIE DUST...
## *Another Adventure With Nana*

PIXIE DUST...
ANOTHER ADVENTURE WITH NANA

Copyright 2014

ISBN 978-0-615-99701-8

# Dedication

This book is dedicated to my family. Beginning with my Dad, Dr. Harry J. Kwantes, who never got to publish the book he had written before he died in January 2013. Next is my Mom, Mrs. Henrietta Kwantes, whose encouragement has always been such a blessing to me! Thanks Mom, I love you! Then to my son, Christopher R. DeHaan, who died way too young. Then to my husband, Bruce; daughter, Jennifer Lynne and her husband Daryl; and my son, Matthew (fondly called "Ooncle Maaattt" by his nieces). Last but not least, to my grandchildren, Ellie, Jana, and Caleb. THEY are the reason for this book! THEY are the reason for the "Pixie Dust" and their belief that it works!

# PIXIE DUST...
## ANOTHER ADVENTURE WITH NANA

Once upon a time in a land not so far away, lived a family. Part of this family; Granddad, Nana, and uncle Matt (affectionately called "Ooncle Maatt" by his nieces) lived in Tuscaloosa, Alabama.

The rest of this family-Jennifer and her husband Daryl, along with their children; Ellie, Jana, and Caleb lived in the city of Rock Spring, Georgia.

These families got to visit each other often and even made special adventures and memories together. Some of these adventures were real and some of them were pretend or make believe.

They traveled together by car to places like Michigan to visit their relatives that live there. They had to travel through many states to get there.

They even got to see windmills that power electricity as they drove through the state of Indiana. At night they looked like tiny red lights all in a row, almost like a string of Christmas lights. It was amazing!

It took a long time to get to Michigan, and when they got there it was snowing.

After they rested, they got to go outside and play in the snow.  They made snow angels and even a small snowman. Oh what fun they had!

One of their favorite places they would go on one of their pretend adventures was to China.  Nana even made special hats out of paper plates for them all to wear, and Ellie made tickets so they could get on the airplane, train, and the boat.

To go on this adventure, they had to travel in many ways. They first had to go by car to get to the airport to get on the plane.

They also had to travel by boat, train, and helicopter. What an adventure it was!

When they could not get together in person, they would talk together by telephone.

This is the story about one visit and a special adventure where our Pixie Dust all started. Ellie and Jana both loved ballet, fairies, and playing make believe.

Caleb was just a toddler at this time, so he spent most of his time just watching and laughing with his sisters.

One day, Nana, Granddad, and Uncle Matt went by car to visit Ellie, Jana, and Caleb at their house.

They played together all day and had all kinds of adventures, including their favorite trip to China. What fun they had!

As the day went along, the girls started to get tired and seemed to cry for just about anything. Ellie and Jana were not happy and the crying got louder and louder and lasted longer and longer.

Even their Mom trying to comfort them by singing the girls favorite song, "Mommy Love", did not help. Pretty soon everyone was sad and also tired of the crying. Even Caleb didn't know what to think.

Then, all of a sudden, Nana had an idea! Maybe she had an answer to stop the crying! She decided to at least try.

"Hey, Ellie and Jana." said Nana. "Do you need some Pixie Dust?"

Instantly, both girls stopped crying and ran over to the couch where Nana was sitting and dropped to their knees in front of her.

"What Nana?" said Ellie, "Do YOU have Pixie Dust?"

"I sure do!" said Nana. Nana then took her hand and reached into her pants pocket.

"Hey, Jana, come here! Nana has Pixie Dust!" Both girls sat at Nana's feet with eyes wide open and mouths dropped wide open waiting to see what Nana had.

"Okay girls, what color Pixie Dust do you need?" asked Nana as she slowly pulled her closed hand out of her pocket.

"I need pink!" said Ellie.

"I need blue!" said Jana.

"Okay, are you ready? Can you show Nana where your boo-boo is?" asked Nana.

Immediately both Ellie and Jana searched for and then pointed to where their boo-boo was. Then it happened!

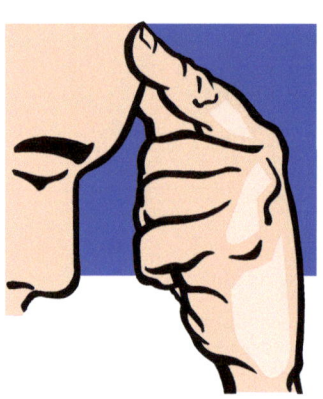 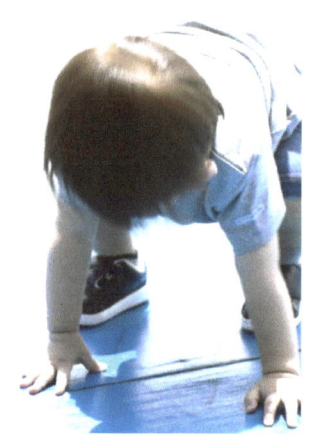

"Ready?" asked Nana. Both girls nodded their heads in excitement and anticipation.

Nana slowly opened her hand and with a gentle breath blew the Pixie Dust towards their boo-boo.

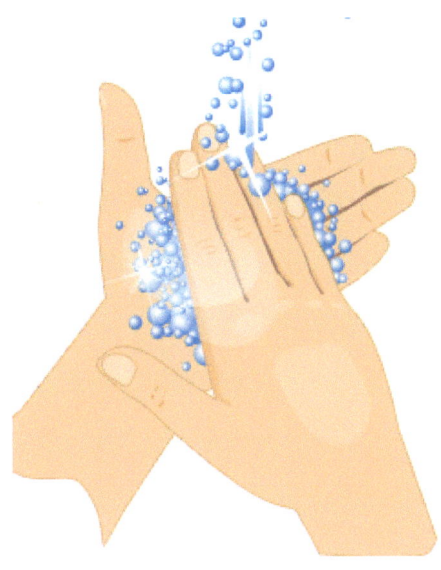

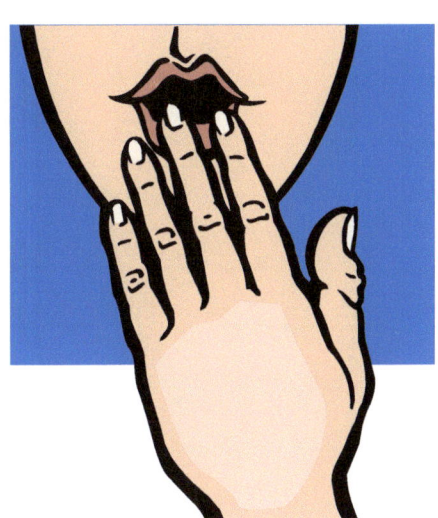

Nana blew pink Pixie Dust to Ellie.

Nana blew blue Pixie Dust to Jana.

Ellie's and Jana's mouths flew open and their eyes got even wider. They both jumped up and hugged Nana and Granddad around the neck.

"Oh Nana!  Nyanks Nana, nyanks!  I am better!"  said Ellie and Jana.  Then off they went to play again, happy once again, and not crying anymore!

""Momma, what in the world?" said Jennifer. "How did you know THAT would work?"

"I didn't know that it would, but it worked!" said Nana smiling.  The adults all laughed and shook their heads at what had just happened.  Even little Caleb was smiling now that the crying had stopped.

"I just cannot believe it, Momma.  You need to keep THAT handy!" said Jennifer smiling.

Soon it was time for Nana, Granddad, and Uncle Matt to go back to their home in Alabama. Everyone hugged each other and life went on as usual.

Several times after this day, Nana would get a telephone call from Jennifer, Ellie, or Jana.

"Hey, Momma, can you talk with Jana?" asked Jennifer.
"Sure, Jennifer." said Nana.

Jennifer put Jana on speaker phone so Nana could hear Jana better.

"Nana, I REALLY REALLY need some blue Pixie Dust!" cried Jana.

"Honey, what is wrong?" asked Nana.

"I went to the Dentist, and my new teeth REALLY REALLY hurt. Can I have some blue Pixie Dust please?" cried Jana on the telephone.

"Okay, Jana. Did you say blue? Yes, I still have some. Are you ready?" asked Nana.

Jennifer told Nana that Jana was nodding her head.

"Here it comes!  Pffft." as Nana ever so gently blew into the telephone sending the blue Pixie Dust to Jana.

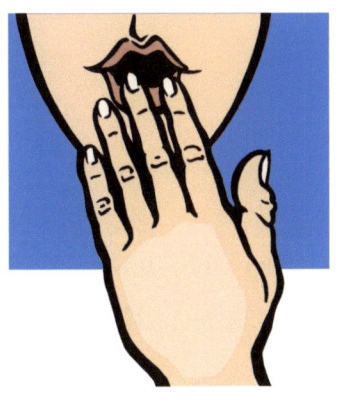 

"Oh, Nana!  Nyanks!  I feel better!" said Jana.  "I love you, Nana!"

"Oh, you are so welcome, Jana, I love you too."  said Nana smiling.

"Well, Momma, it worked again!  Go figure!" said Jennifer.  "I love you, Momma!"

"I love you too, Jennifer."  said Nana.

A few more days went by and the telephone rang again. "Hello?" said Nana.

"Nana, this is Ellie. Nana, I really need some Pixie Dust." said Ellie crying, "I have a boo-boo and it hurts really really bad."

"Okay, Ellie, what color do you need?" asked Nana.
"Do you have any pink left over Nana?" asked Ellie, still crying.

"Let me check for you, Ellie. Oh yes, I do have some pink! Are you ready? Where is your boo-boo?" asked Nana.

Nana gave Ellie time to pinpoint where her boo-boo was and then ever so gently blew the pink Pixie Dust into the telephone for Ellie.

"Oh Nana, I love you! It worked, I feel better! Nyanks! Talk to you later, Nana." said Ellie, no longer crying. Nana could almost see the smile on Ellie's face.

"Hey, Momma. This beats everything, but I'm glad it works! Love you Momma." said Jennifer.
"I love you too, Jennifer." said Nana.

Many more times, Jennifer or one of the girls, and even once Caleb called wanting to know if Nana still had enough Pixie Dust so she could send them some. Nana would tell them to point to their boo-boo, ask what color they needed and ever so gently blow the Pixie Dust through the telephone to them. It always seemed to help them feel better.

This always brought a smile to Nana's face knowing that even though she was far away, she could help her grandchildren feel better.

Then something happened.  Nana got very sick and had to go to the hospital.

She had pneumonia and was very very sick. She looked at Granddad and said to him, "I need some Pixie Dust." as tears rolled down her face.

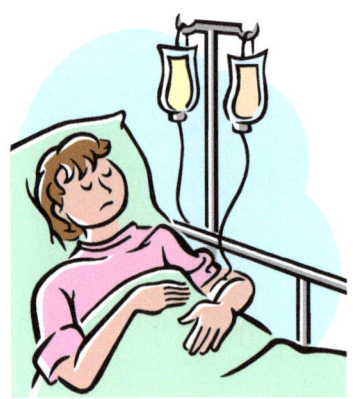

"I'll take care of it!' said Granddad as he bent over and kissed her on the forehead.

Pretty soon the telephone rang in Nana's hospital room.
"Hello?" said Nana very weakly.

"Hey Nana? This is Ellie. Mommy and Granddad told me you are sick and in the hospital." said Ellie.

"Yes, Ellie. I am in the hospital and very sick." said Nana.

"I have some pink Pixie Dust for you, Nana!" said Ellie. The next sound Nana heard was a long hard blow into the telephone. Ellie was blowing her Pixie Dust to Nana to help her feel better.

"Nana, I am praying for you. I hope my pink Pixie Dust helps you feel better! I love you, Nana!" said Ellie.

"Oh, Nyanks Ellie! It will. I love you too!" said Nana smiling with tears running down her face.

"Nana, here is Jana. She wants to talk to you too. Bye Nana!" said Ellie.

"Hey, Nana. I love you! I have Pixie Dust for you too, what color do you want Nana?" asked Jana.

"How about blue?" asked Nana. The next sound Nana heard was a gently steady blowing into the telephone. Jana was sharing her Pixie Dust with Nana hoping it would help Nana feel better.

"I love you, Nana! I pray for you! Bye Nana!" said Jana.

Again, tears came down Nana's face, but she was not sad she had a smile on her face.

Nana had no idea why the Pixie Dust "worked" with the girls, her daughter, and now even herself!

When any of the nurses or helpers came into Nana's room, she shared with them the story of the Pixie Dust. After she told them, they cried, smiled, or said, "Wow! That's unreal!"

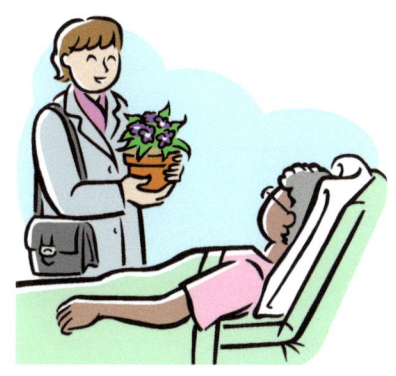

Nana got better and was able to go back home after a few days in the hospital.

Nana decided that she wanted to share the story of the Pixie Dust with more people. So she started to write down the story to share with others.

So, what is the secret of the Pixie Dust?  Nana says that Pixie Dust cannot be seen with your eyes.  You cannot feel Pixie Dust with your hands.  It takes knowing that you need something or Someone to help you and then believing it will work.  It also means to have enough of it, you have to share it with others.  It will always be there when you need it and you will not run out of it either.

Why? Nana says that Pixie Dust is made up of love, prayer, and faith.  Just like in The Bible it tells us,

*"To have faith is to be sure of the things we hope for, to be certain of the things we cannot see…it is by faith that we understand."  Hebrews 11:1 & 3a (Good News Bible)*

Nana knows that Ellie and Jana understand this faith. They continue to ask Nana for Pixie Dust. Sometimes, they will even send some to Nana, Granddad, and Uncle Matt. They also pray for Nana and love her. Nana does the same for them and little Caleb.

Nana plans to send anyone who needs a little Pixie Dust some when they need it as well as continue to tell the story of the Pixie Dust to anyone who needs to hear it!

# ABOUT THE AUTHOR

Henriette M. "Mickey" DeHaan has been married to her husband Bruce for almost 40 years.

"Mickey" is her nickname given to her by her Dad many years ago, after his sister Mary.

She is a retired nurse after 30+ years and currently works part-time for a local business.

She has three children: Jennifer Lynne, Matthew, and Christopher Reuben-who is in Heaven.

She has three grandchildren: Ellie, Jana, and Caleb.

Her hobbies include: Photography, sewing,, writing, & spending time with her family & grandchildren.

She is an active member of her church.  She has gone on many short-term mission trips (both overseas and stateside).  She also volunteers when she can at the Ministry of The Wings of Grace Relief Center.

~~~~~~~~~

This is her first book Mickey has written.  She has her rough manuscript ready for a second book, in which she shares about the journey she and her family went through when Christopher died.

~~~~~

"It is my desire, that this book somehow minister to those who find themselves either facing a valley, are in the midst of a valley, or coming out of a valley.  If you find yourself in any of these, I pray this book will give you some encouragement.  God bless you and thanks for buying and reading my book!" -*Mickey*

Mickey & her family from left to right:
Top: Son-in-law Daryl, Bruce, Matthew
Middle: Caleb, Jennifer Lynne, Mickey
Bottom: Ellie & Jana